First edition 2002

Library of Congress Cataloging-in-Publication Data

Spires, Elizabeth.
The big meow / Elizabeth Spires ; illustrated by Cynthia Jabar. —1st ed.
p. cm.
Summary: Little Cat bothers the other cats with his loud meow, but it comes
in handy when they are chased by a nasty bulldog.
ISBN 0-7636-0679-0
[1. Cats—Fiction. 2. Noise—Fiction.
3. Dogs—Fiction.] I. Jabar, Cynthia, ill. II. Title.
PZ7.S7568 Bi 2001
[E]—dc21 00-037885

2 4 6 8 10 9 7 5 3 1

Printed in Hong Kong

This book was typeset in Humana Sans.
The illustrations were done in acrylic.

Candlewick Press
2067 Massachusetts Avenue
Cambridge, Massachusetts 02140

visit us at www.candlewick.com

The Big
MEOW

For Ann and Jumper
E. S.

For my mum, the bravest of all
C. J.

The Big MEOW

Elizabeth Spires   illustrated by Cynthia Jabar

CANDLEWICK PRESS

CAMBRIDGE, MASSACHUSETTS

Little Cat had a big meow. It was loud as a lion's roar. When Little Cat meowed, the trees quivered and shivered all over town.

MEOW

"Little Cat, Little Cat, go away! Scat!" said the other cats. "Your meow makes the sidewalk shake. It gives us a headache. Can't you learn to pipe down?"

So Little Cat ran home and asked his mother, "Is my meow a bother to you and to Father?"

"Oh no, Catkin," said his mother. "We're proud of your meow, so big and so loud. It's purrr-fect!"

"But HOW did I get such a big MEOW?" he asked.

And Little Cat's mother said, "The ME- is from me, and the -OW is from your father, Tom Cat. His yowling used to keep the neighborhood up all night."

Little Cat felt better after that.
He ran back to the other cats and said,
"MEOW! Please let me play. My mother says
my meow makes her day."

But the other cats said,
"Little Cat, Little Cat, go away! Scat!"

"Your meow wakes us up from our catnaps."

"It scares off the catbirds in the catalpa tree."

"Your meow is one big CAT-astrophe!"

This time Little Cat ran to his father. "Father, is my meow a bother to you and to Mother?"

"Son," answered Tom Cat, "I wouldn't trade your meow for a year of catfish dinners. You remind me of myself when I was just a ball of fluff. So go show those cats you're proud of your stuff!"

With that, Little Cat
let out another big meow.

It grew and grew until it was big as a rain cloud.

"Little Cat, Little Cat, look what you've done!" the other cats cried. "Your big meow just swallowed the sun!"

"I'm sorry," said Little Cat. "If I stop meowing, will you let me play?"

MEO

"Little Cat, we're NEVER going to play with you!
Not today, not tomorrow, not the day after that!
Now scat!"

So Little Cat spent the morning alone under the porch, practicing his meows. He made them bright.

He made them pale.

EOOOOWWWWW

He made them into a song, like notes on a scale, then stretched them out until they were very, very long.

me meowww

Then, tired out from so much meowing,
Little Cat fell asleep and had a dream.
In his dream, a big meow was chasing *him*!

MEOW

But it wasn't a dream at all.

"Little Cat, wake up!" the other cats cried.
"A nasty bulldog named Bruno is chasing us,
and we need a place to hide."

"Little Cat," they begged,
"We're sorry we were mean today.
We're sorry we wouldn't play.
Please, please, scare Bruno away!"

"GROWL!" snarled Bruno,
a crazy gleam in his eye.
"GROWLL! GROWLLL!"

"If you cats don't come out of there,
I'm coming in!" he threatened.

Little Cat was afraid,
but a tiny voice
inside him said,
BE BRAVE.

So Little Cat stepped outside and looked Bruno straight in the eye.

"Bruno, sir," said Little Cat politely, "no bullies allowed. You'll have to leave now. If you don't, I'll let loose with my big meow."

Bruno let out a laugh that almost split him in half.

"An itty-bitty thing like you is going to tell ME what to do?" laughed Bruno. "Why, what a delicious snack you'll make. A tasty tidbit before I have that bunch of quivering cowards for lunch!"

Little Cat closed his eyes and imagined his BIGGEST meow. But he was shaking so hard only a tiny MEOW came out.

Bruno giggled. "THAT was your big meow? Why, I've heard mice squeak louder than that."

Little Cat tried again. "MEOW."

Bruno grinned. "If that was your BIGGEST meow, I don't have much to worry about."

The bulldog stepped closer and snapped his jaws. Then he boxed Little Cat's ears with his great big paws.

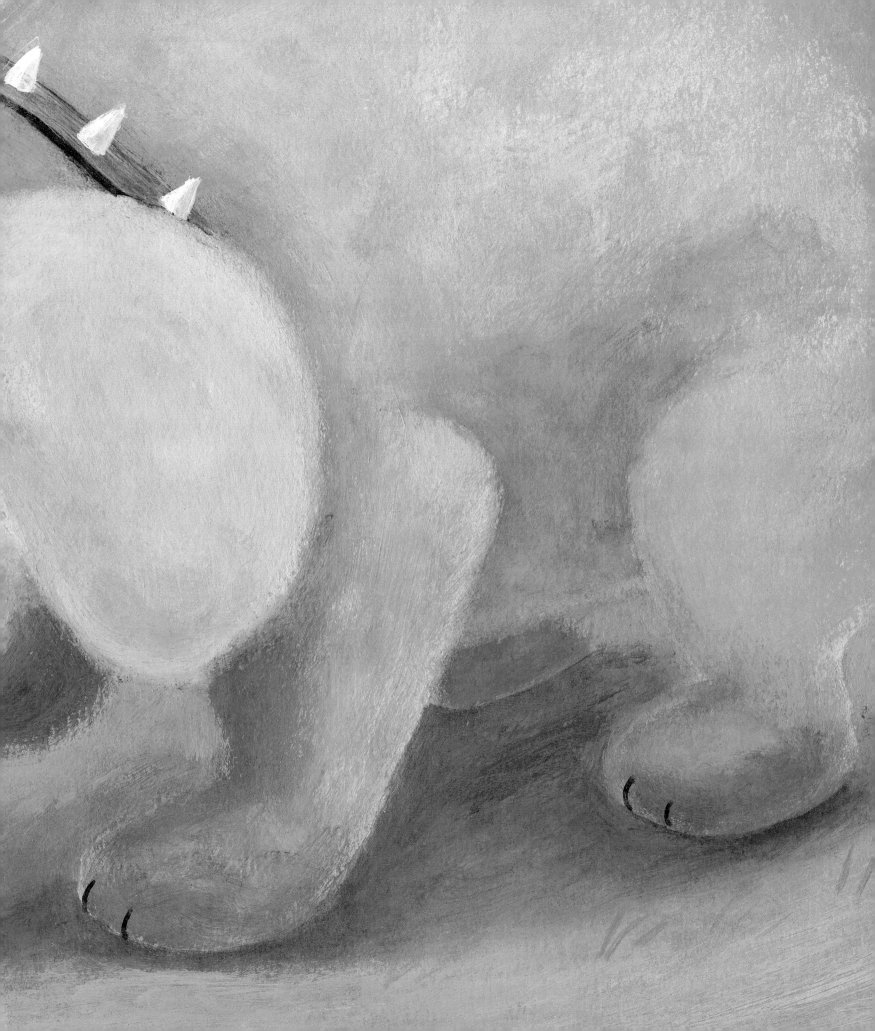

That did it! Little Cat was angry now.
He took a deep breath and . . .

MEO

MEC

MEC

W!

Little Cat's first meow blew Bruno over like a paper doll.

W!

Little Cat's second meow threw
Bruno against the house and pinned him there, flat as a pancake.

OW!

Little Cat's third meow catapulted
Bruno over the horizon, clear into the next town.

"Little Cat, that was terrific! That was great!" cheered the other cats. "Now how about chasing ALL the dogs away?"

But Little Cat just smiled and said, "I think I'll save that for another day. I'm just a little cat who wants to play. That's the only thing I wanted to do today."

"Then let's play!" the other cats yelled.

And with that, Little Cat let out his best and happiest meow. A meow so big and so loud it ends our story here and now—